DOZEY DOG
AND
KITTY KATNAP

STOCKWELL
PUBLISHERS SINCE 1898

Linda Tarry

Published in 2022 by
Linda Tarry in association with
Arthur H Stockwell Ltd
West Wing Studios
Unit 166, The Mall
Luton, Bedfordshire
ahstockwell.co.uk

British Library Cataloguing-in-Publication Data
A catalogue record for this book is available
from the British Library.
ISBN: 9781739730307

All characters appearing in this work are
fictitious. Any resemblance to real persons,
living or dead, is purely coincidental.

To my grandchildren, my inspiration

Chapter 1

Hannah was in her bedroom, clearing out her wardrobe. She had just had her fourteenth birthday and was trying to make room for the new clothes she had received as part of her birthday presents.

"There you are!" she exclaimed. "I've been looking for you."

At the bottom of the wardrobe lay a fluffy toy dog. She pulled him out and cuddled him.

"Dozey," she whispered into his fur, "I've missed you, but I think it is time I gave you to my younger cousins, Lina and Jessa."

On her next visit to her cousins' house, Hannah pulled Lina (the elder of the two sisters) to one side and said, "I want to give you this." And she pushed Dozey Dog into Lina's hands.

"Oh!" said Lina. "I already have cuddly toys. I really do not need any more!"

"I know," said Hannah, "but believe me when I tell you this one is special!"

"Really?" said Lina, slightly confused.

"Yes," said Hannah, "and you must promise me: whatever happens, take Jessa with you."

"Why?" asked Lina.

"Wait and see," said Hannah, laughing, "and you can tell me about it next time I see you."

Lina didn't want to upset her big cousin, so she took Dozey Dog upstairs and put him on her bed.

She looked at him closely and thought, 'He looks old and worn, but I will give him a brush and make his fur shiny again.'

With that she left her bedroom and went downstairs to enjoy the rest of her cousin's visit.

Later that night when Lina was just about to fall asleep she felt a tickle on her cheek. She brushed it off and then it happened again. She opened her eyes and sat up. Staring back at her was Dozey Dog.

"Hello, Lina," he said. "I've come to take you to Dreamland!"

"What?" said Lina, not believing what she was seeing or hearing.

"I'm Dozey Dog and Hannah asked me to take you and your sister, Jessa, to Dreamland. Now let's wake her up as we have no time to waste."

A little startled, Lina went over to her sister's bed and gently shook her. Jessa sat up and rubbed her eyes.

"What is it, Lina?" asked Jessa grumpily as she had been fast asleep.

"You are never going to believe this, Jessa. Please don't make a loud noise, but look!"

Peering through Lina's legs Dozey waved his paw and said, "Hello, Jessa. I'm Dozey Dog."

Jessa opened her mouth and closed it again. Dozey then walked around and stood in front of Jessa.

He spoke softly, saying, "Hannah sent me to take you both to Dreamland. Are you ready to come with me?"

Jessa thought about it for a moment and then giggled and said, "Yes please."

"Right," said Dozey, "let's go and sit on Lina's quilt on her bed and then we need to say the magic words."

They all sat on the bed and waited for Dozey to say the words.

"Right – repeat after me," he said.

<blockquote>
"Rub your nose,

Wiggle your toes,

Do something funny

Like tickle your tummy,

Close your eyes,

Then comes the surprise."
</blockquote>

Lina and Jessa repeated the words as well as rubbing their noses and wiggling their toes, and they laughed when they tickled each other's tummies.

When they closed their eyes, the quilt they were sitting on suddenly lifted off the bed and flew out of the open window. They all clung on tightly to the quilt, which continued to fly high into the sky. The stars were out and sparkling and the moon was shining bright.

Suddenly they could see the face of the moon and were surprised when he suddenly laughed loudly and said, "Hello, Lina and Jessa. I see you have fine weather to travel to Dreamland. I hope the rain stays away – I do not want you to get wet. Enjoy yourselves. Kitty Katnap is waiting for you."

Lina and Jessa were so surprised the moon had just spoken to them. They waved to the moon and shouted, "Thank you."

"Who is Kitty Katnap?" they asked Dozey Dog.

At that moment the quilt swooped down and landed by a tree just outside great big gates with a big sign on top of it saying

'WELCOME TO DREAMLAND'

A moment later they saw a cat come out from behind the tree.

"Hello, Dozey," she said. "I'm glad you could come tonight. The clouds are out having fun – I hope you can join them. And I see you have brought some friends with you!"

Dozey introduced Lina and Jessa to Kitty and then they all walked towards the big gates. In the next moment Kitty climbed the gates and pushed her paw into the keyhole. The gates slowly opened up and they all walked through.

Lina grabbed Jessa's hand, both of them feeling excited and wondering what might happen next.

As they looked around they saw houses of many colours and different shapes. Some were round, some were square and some were triangular.

Living in the houses were bubble people. They were of all different colours – red, blue, orange, yellow, green, purple ... They had bodies, arms and legs, hands and feet, head and faces. Lina thought they looked like they were made out of balloons. Jessa waved to some that had appeared in their doorways and they waved back and smiled at her.

They carried on walking through the town, and as they turned a corner they couldn't believe what they saw: all around them were the bubble people playing with clouds.

A red bubble person asked Lina and Jessa if they would like to join in.

"What do we have to do?" asked Lina.

"Please call me Redbubble," said the bubble person. "All you have to do is ask a cloud to change into anything you want, and it will do so."

Jessa thought for a moment and then called to the cloud, "Please change into a unicorn!"

The cloud suddenly became a unicorn.

Jessa ran to it and climbed on the cloud, and in the next minute the cloud unicorn was flying around with her on its back.

Lina looked on surprised at what her sister had just done. Not wanting to miss out, she said to another cloud, "Please change into a giraffe."

The cloud changed and Lina did the same as Jessa: she climbed on the cloud giraffe, which also flew her around. The girls giggled and shouted to each other. What fun this was!

Eventually the clouds put them back on the ground and flew away.

Dozey, who had been watching them, said, "I think it's time we left now to go home."

"Oh no!" said the girls together. "We are having so much fun – please, Dozey, let us stay a little longer!"

Orangebubble said, "Come inside for some hot chocolate and cookies before you go?"

"All right," said Dozey, "then we really must be on our way."

They all followed Orangebubble to his house, which was purple and round. As they entered they noticed everything in the house was round, including the table and chairs, the comfy sofa and the TV. They all drank hot chocolate and ate cookies.

"This is purrfect!" said Kitty, and started softly singing.

"Dreamland is the place to be.
It's full of possibilities.
Lina and Jessa had fun
But their time here has only just begun.

"Please come back tomorrow night,
Though you might be scared
And have a fright!
Scaryland is—"

But before she could finish the girls asked, "What is Scaryland, Kitty?"

"Well," said Kitty, "if you are good, I am sure Dozey will bring you back tomorrow night and show you some of the scary parts to Dreamland, but you will have to be brave to go there. Do you think you are ready for that?"

Lina and Jessa both looked at each other with wide eyes and shouted at the same time, "Yes!"

As they climbed on the quilt, which they had left by Kitty Katnap's tree, they watched her lock the gates to Dreamland by putting her paw back in the keyhole.

The quilt took off, carrying Lina, Jessa and Dozey Dog. Jessa yawned, suddenly feeling tired. They passed the moon, who smiled and waved to them, and in the next moment they were back on Lina's bed.

Dozey took Jessa back to her bed and she fell immediately to sleep. He then climbed back on Lina's bed and turned back into a soft furry toy. Lina put him next to her on her pillow and, as she thought about her time in Dreamland, fell into a deep sleep.

The next day Hannah came to visit with her brother, Matt.

She whispered to Lina, "Did you have fun with Dozey Dog last night?"

Lina nodded and went on to tell her big cousin all about their adventure, but Hannah just but her finger to her lips, said sh-h-h-h-h and winked. "There will be more trips out with Dozey. Just have fun," she said.

Lina sat there thinking for a moment. She just couldn't wait for bedtime to see what would happen next in Dreamland or Scaryland.

Chapter 2

Matt was fed up. It was raining and his plans to go on a bike ride with his friends had been cancelled. He had just finished playing a game on his computer and was missing his older sister, Hannah.

'She is so lucky,' he thought to himself. 'She is allowed out late with her friends.'

At that moment Matt's mum appeared at his bedroom door.

"Matt, pack an overnight bag. You are going to stay the night with your auntie, uncle and cousins. Your dad and I are going out for the evening and Hannah is sleeping over at Lily's."

"OK, Mum," said Matt. Secretly he was happy. "I wonder if those cousins of mine are going to Dreamland with Dozey Dog? Maybe they will take me with them? Dozey used to take me with Hannah!"

"Don't forget your rain jacket, Matt," said his mum, "It's still raining."

At his auntie and uncle's house Matt was greeted by his younger cousins, Lina and Jessa. They were so excited to see him and dragged him off to show him where he was sleeping.

Once they were away from the grown-ups Lina couldn't wait to tell him about their visit to Dreamland.

"Tonight, Matt, we are going to visit Scaryland. Will you come with us? Jessa wants to go, but I think having her big cousin with us will make her feel less scared, if you know what I mean!"

"That will be fun," said Matt. "I've missed going out with Dozey. I hope he will let me come and not think I'm too old."

Lina laughed. "It's OK – Jessa has already asked him and he is looking forward to seeing you again."

It was still raining when they all went to bed, so they all secretly put their rain jackets under their pillows and wellies under their beds.

As they were drifting off to sleep Lina felt the familiar paw of Dozey Dog on her cheek. She sat up.

"Hello, Dozey. Are we going to Scaryland?"

"Yes," said Dozey, "but first we must wake up Jessa and Matt."

It wasn't long before Lina, Jessa and Matt were sitting on Lina's quilt in their pyjamas, raincoats and wellies.

"Now for the magic words – I hope you remember them, Matt?" said Dozey.

"I do," said Matt.

They all said together,

>"Rub your nose,
>
>Wiggle your toes,
>
>Do something funny
>
>Like tickle your tummy,
>
>Close your eyes,
>
>Then comes the surprise."

Lina, Jessa and Matt said the words as well as rubbing their noses and wiggling their toes, and they all laughed when they tickled each other's tummies.

The quilt rose up from the bed and flew out of the open window. Lina tucked Dozey into the pocket in her jacket to keep him dry from the rain. It was raining so hard the clouds covered the moon and no stars were shining. Yet before they knew it they landed outside the familiar gates of Dreamland. Kitty Katnap was waiting for them.

"It's lovely to see you all again – especially you, Matt," said Kitty.

"You too, Kitty," grinned Matt.

It had finally stopped raining, so the quilt flew up to Kitty's tree and hung from a branch to dry off.

Kitty put her paw into the keyhole of the gates of Dreamland and they slowly opened.

This time it was different from their last visit: it was very gloomy. It was not dark, but there was no sunshine.

"What's happened?" cried Jessa, grabbing Matt's hand.

"We are in Scaryland," said Kitty.

Lina, Jessa and Matt stood there for a minute wide-eyed, not one of them saying a word.

"Come on," said Dozey, "or it will be time to go back."

They all crept forward slowly. As luck would have it, Dozey had brought a torch with him, and he turned it on so they could see where they were going.

It was very quiet and misty. They could barely see what was in front of them. Then they heard a loud 'crunch crunch', followed by a 'thump thump' sound.

They all stopped and stood very still.

'Crunch crunch, thump thump' came the sound again.

Then they heard, "Where are they? Grrrrr!"

Suddenly a fluffy green monster appeared out of the bushes. He had four eyes and pointy teeth.

Lina and Jessa screamed in fright and the fluffy green monster screamed back at them.

Matt stepped forward and spoke to the monster: "Hello. My name is Matt. Who are you?"

The monster was so surprised someone had spoken to him he stopped screaming and suddenly burst into tears.

Jessa couldn't bear to see him crying. She lost all her fear and ran and gave him a big hug.

"What's the matter, fluffy green monster? Do you have a name?" she asked.

The monster was trying with all his might to stop crying, but the tears just kept on coming.

He did manage to mumble that his name was Flumpy.

Lina went over to Flumpy and took hold of the monster's claw-like hand.

"My name is Lina. This is my sister, Jessa, my cousin Matt and Dozey Dog and Kitty Katnap."

They all waved their hands and paws.

Flumpy looked at them all and sighed. "Why are you all being so kind to me? I'm a fluffy green monster with four eyes and pointy teeth. I scare people."

"I was scared at first," said Jessa, "but then I realised you were just different from me and that's nothing to be scared of."

Matt stepped forward and spoke softly: "You know what, Flumpy – it's OK to be different. I go to a big school now and if I do something different they all tease me; so do you know what I do?"

"No," said Flumpy, "what do you do?"

"I laugh with them. Sometimes I even make the jokes and they laugh with me."

"Do you?"said Flumpy.

"We all do!" said Lina, "And anyway I like different. It's better than all being the same. That is so-o-o-o-o boring. Different people, things and green fluffy monsters are far more interesting."

Flumpy smiled showing all his pointy teeth, and the tears stopped flowing.

"Thank you, but I also have to wear glasses. Will you still like me then?"

"Of course we will!" said Matt. "In case you haven't noticed, I wear them too."

Flumpy giggled. "Oh yes, but I've lost mine."

Flumpy and the children hadn't noticed that Dozey and Kitty had disappeared. Then they all froze on the spot as they heard the bushes rustling.

Jessa whispered to herself, "Be brave. Don't be scared. But watch out as you don't know who is there."

At that moment Dozey and Kitty appeared carrying a huge pair of glasses with four lenses for each one of Flumpy's eyes.

"I believe these are yours!" said Dozey. "Now come on, children – we must get back home now."

Flumpy took the glasses and put them on.

"I can see you all clearly now. Thanks."

The fluffy green monster did look funny with his enormous glasses. Dozey, Kitty and the children all looked at each other and they couldn't help it – they burst out laughing. Flumpy looked at them all laughing, but this time instead of crying he laughed too.

As they all started to walk away, Flumpy called after them: "What shall I do now? I can't stay in Scaryland now I am happy."

"Come back to Dreamland with me," said Kitty Katnap. "When you feel in a bad mood or grumpy you can come back to Scaryland until you feel better again. You will make friends in Dreamland; and everyone is different there, so you will feel at home."

Flumpy suddenly grabbed hold of Kitty and gave her a great big fluffy-green-monster hug.

Everyone laughed and made their way back to the big gate.

"I'm sorry, children – there is no time for milk and cookies tonight as we are running late. Let's see if the quilt has finished drying," said Dozey.

At the gate Flumpy hugged Lina, Jessa, Matt and Dozey. Kitty Katnap then closed the big gate and locked it with her paw.

The quilt, now dry, came floating down and they all sat on it ready for their journey home.

"Come back soon," said Kitty. "I believe the lazy chip wants to meet you."

"The lazy chip? What does it do?" asked Lina.

"Nothing much!" said Kitty, and they all laughed.

It had stopped raining, so they were dry and warm when they returned home. They were all feeling very sleepy.

Thank you for coming with us, Matt. I was scared, but I knew you would take care of us," said Jessa.

"I had fun. Thank you for letting me come – it was really good to see Dozey Dog and Kitty Katnap again. I can't wait to tell Hannah."

They all went to bed, and Dozey climbed in with Lina and became a soft toy again.

THE END

Ingram Content Group UK Ltd.
Milton Keynes UK
UKHW050633060423
419642UK00003B/10

9 781739 730307